William Alden

Lines, rhymes or poetry as you choose to call them

William Alden

Lines, rhymes or poetry as you choose to call them

ISBN/EAN: 9783337272029

Printed in Europe, USA, Canada, Australia, Japan

Cover: Foto ©Andreas Hilbeck / pixelio.de

More available books at **www.hansebooks.com**

LINES

RHYMES, OR POETRY

AS YOU CHOOSE TO CALL THEM

BY

WILLIAM C. ALDEN

CAMBRIDGE

Printed at the Riverside Press

1878

THE author, in allowing these pieces to be given to the public, by a too partial judge, would only say that they were mostly written as occasion or incident called them forth, either at the request or for the pleasure of pleasant companions, by whom, as a matter of course, they would be favorably received, and not with the idea of publication. Should they meet with like approbation from others, no one would be more surprised than himself.

CONTENTS.

FIRST OF THE FLEET.

HE stands upon the farthest land,
  To watch the bark glide swiftly by,
And hope, and fear, go hand in hand;
  Almost a smile, yet half a sigh
    Show in his face the while.

Is this the last I 'll send to sea,
  Or will she wealth and pleasure bring?
Will other eyes her beauties see,
  And other lips her praises sing?
    Say, shall I sigh, or smile?

And shall I other vessels launch,
  And hearts beside my own make glad,
And others' words pronounce them staunch
  And — not drift back, all torn and sad,
    A shattered, hopeless pile?

Thus poets give the world their song,
   The artist's picture meets the eye,
When first they to the world belong,
   They trembling watch the world draw
     nigh,
   Whether to sigh, or smile.

IN UNION SQUARE.

Back from the country summer days,
Back to the city's weary ways,
The hard stone pavement 'neath my feet,
Across the noisy, busy street,
   I went, into the little Square.

No thought of meadows or of streams
Came in my working city dreams,
Amidst the eager, earnest strife,
The struggle and the work of life,
   Where all is toil and care.

Unconsciously I turned my gaze,
To where the fountain throws its sprays,
When lo! no more I seemed to stand
Amid a hurrying city band,
   But back to boyhood's days.

Only a few tall, slender stalks,
" The cat tail," — sought in boyish walks,
A bunch of leaves, a few rank weeds ;
But not a thousand fiery steeds,
    Could take my body back as they,

Took memory back to early years,
Its fill of joys, its foolish tears,
I stood there wrapt in pleasant thought,
The crowd, the noise, the strife, were
        naught —
    I was a *boy* that day.

MY WIFE AND I.

THE rain-drops fall on the outside wall,
　　But we sit in a pleasant glow;
And the gas-light bright, in this winter
　　　　night,
　　Dims not with the sleet or snow.

And we say good-by, both she and I,
　　For the time, to all cares of life;
She holds me true, and I give the due
　　Of trust in my faithful wife.

The love that lies in the other's eyes —
　　Each notes with a swelling heart,
As we loving stand, and hand clasps hand,
　　All burdens of life apart.

The winds may blow, and drift the snow,
　　And storms of care may rage;

We 'll onward move, and together prove
  Our faith in a happy age.

So side by side, whate'er betide,
  We 'll walk our earthward way,
Through gathering cloud, with a spirit
    proud,
  And trust in a better day.

A MIDSUMMER MORNING.

THE eastern sky is all aflame;
The day is breaking;
The darkness flees in very shame,
 Its haunts forsaking.
The mists along the mountain sides are fly-
  ing,
 In waving lines;
The morning breeze awakes with sighing,
 From out the pines.
The robin on the highest tree,
 Calls to its mate,
And carols forth, in merry glee,
 You 're late! you 're late!
The clover in the field, its leaves unfolding,
 Shakes off the dew.
All nature feels a fresher power upholding,
 Its pulses through.

•

The western hills the first bright rays are
  feeling,
  In golden glow;
Adown their sides in wanton warmth they're
  stealing,
  To depths below.
With heated passion upon Mother Earth
  Comes down the sun,
Till in her breast she feels some fresh new
  birth,
  Has just begun;
And languidly beneath his ardent blaze
  She seems to lay,
While fiercer still upon her sends his rays,
  The god of day.

"I KNOW NOT THAT I LOVE THEE."

I KNOW not that I love thee; but I know,
That joy thy presence is, thine absence woe;
When thou art near, there's brightness in
    my heart
That fades to darkness in it when we part.

I know not that I love thee; yet I know,
When thou art absent, time drags sad and
    slow;
I wait impatiently the time to come,
That brings thee back, with light and life,
    to home.

I know not that I love thee; still I know,
The blood runs through my veins with joy-
    ful flow,
When you but take my hand, or smooth
    my hair;
The sun seems shining to me everywhere.

ON APPLEDORE.

O BARREN cliffs, whose fissures wide,
Throw open gateways to the tide,
Where is the charm that evermore,
Brings pleasant thoughts of Appledore?
Like some poor soul, whose faith alone
Stands firm 'midst seas of doubts unknown,
Till time with recompense will bring
The weaker souls round it to cling,

So thou, whose tattered form, unsung,
Has bravely stood since time was young,
Finds that thy worn and wrinkled face,
Wears in our hearts a foremost place;
Upon thy adamantine breast,
The world-worn traveler sinks to rest,
And children turn their steps to thee,
And shout aloud their childish glee.

O pleasant Isle, for the summer while,
In the burning blaze of the sunny days,
Where we hear the splash, where the cool
      seas dash,
In the clear bright sheen of the ocean
      green,
On the broken shore of Appledore.

We silent stand, when the ocean grand,
The bold rocks lave with its foam-crest
      wave,
With the smothered power, that but waits
      the hour,
Of the fierce wind squall, and the storm-
      king's call,
To burst as of yore on Appledore.

Or we shout aloud, as the great waves
      proud,
Throw their crooked length, with their
      gathered strength,
And spring on high, and the foam flakes
      fly,

Then crouch them back, for a fresh attack,
With their angry roar, on Appledore.

Or in moonlit nights, watch the changing
    sights :
The golden seas, in the rippling breeze,
Or the shadows change, in their varying
    range,
Or the silver fleece, of the clouds in peace,
That with white wings soar, o'er Apple-
    dore.

In the wintry day, when we far off stray,
'Mid the city's sights, or in dreamy nights,
Will our memory fill, with a joyous thrill
Of the past delight, in the island bright,
We have felt before at Appledore.

THE BABE'S FIRST WALK.

I HEARD the music of the baby's voice
Outside the door, and as I stepped within,
The pleased face turned to me, as one she
      loved,
And gladness shone from out those sweet
      blue eyes.
Go — go to him, the nurse spoke to the
      child ;
And she, with faith that she could do as
      bid,
Stretched forth her little arms, and started
      on,
While earnest effort filled the tiny frame ;
And swaying now to this side, then to that
Now almost stopping on the tedious way,
Yet always smiling, as she tottered on,
She gained my side, and, as I stooped, with
      joyful shout,

She threw her longing arms around my
    neck,
And pressed her soft, dear face to mine with
    sweet content,
Then crowed with joy, as I laughed in de-
    light.

THE McMILLAN HOUSE,

BENEATH the branches of great spreading
    elms,
  A white, low-studded inn, of olden days,
Placed in the fairest spot of Nature's
    realms,
    To tempt the painter's brush, or poet's
    lays.

Upon the very summit of the hill
    That skirts the meadows of the Saco's
    stream,
That gives grand views, our memories to
    fill,
    In after years to open like a dream.

With wide-spread lawn, where soft, fresh
        grasses meet,
    'Neath graceful locust, elm, and maple
        shade,
The tread of tourists or of loiterers' feet,
    And restlessness to quiet is betrayed.

Fit place the weary worker's brain to rest,
    The tired limbs to stretch in sweet re-
        pose,
When every glance with some fair view is
        blest,
    To watch the early dawn, or day's soft
        close.

And here we throw our working harness
        down,
    And idly pass the still, delicious hours;
Trouble and care in pleasant reveries drown,
    And toil no more than do the grass
        and flowers.

THE SEA.

The sea, the sea! is singing in my ears:
I hear its murmuring on the pebbly sand;
In lithe and crested form it gently breaks,
And on its shining edge there seems to
     stand,
Some fair sweet Spirit, bidding me to come.

The sea, the sea! is ringing in my ears:
In sharp, short waves, it throws its strength
     away;
I hear its dashing on the stony shore,
And still there standing, mid the scattered
     spray,
That Spirit calls me, as if 't were my home.

The sea, the sea! is thundering in my ears:
I hear its roaring on the rock-bound coast,
In mighty billows, thrown by unseen power,
And still there beckoning faithful at its post,
I see that Spirit in the whitened foam.

ON CHOCORUA PEAK.

WE ask no legends of thy rugged peak —
Ere man had learned thy hidden paths to
    seek,
Ages had rolled, nor man, nor beast, had
    trod,
Thy rocky cliffs, work of Almighty God.

What are our legends to thy untold tales,
When heaving matter formed thy rocks and
    vales?
Peace to our lips before this sealed book,
And gaze with humble heart, and awe-
    struck look.

"BE NOT AFRAID."

Be not afraid; but come with expectation
Of pleasant greeting shining in thy face,
And leave the memory of thy visit with me,
To gild the dimness of this busy place.

Be not afraid; except that thy sweet pres-
      ence,
Might stir too strong a feeling in my heart;
That feeling all *too* strong, the pleasure of
      thy coming,
I 'd wake, to find it only pain to part.

Be not afraid; I 'd greet thee at thy coming,
As autumn flowers, chilled in October
      night,
Greet the first rays of the bright sun rising,
Drink in its warmth, though dazzled at the
      sight.

WOODLAND MEMORIES.

'T is but a little piece of bark,
  From off that white birch tree ;
Yet pleasant memories of the past,
  It calleth up to me.

The graceful waving boughs o'erhead,
  The moss-grown rocks below,
The fragrance of arbutus flowers,
  Yet moistened by the snow.

The rugged mountains, slumbering near,
  The sound of running streams,
The far off lake that through the tops,
  Of distant forests gleams.

The violet dressed in heaven's own blue,
  The fern leaves spread above,

The noise of winds, the songs of birds,
  The thousand things I love.

Ah me ! that little piece of bark ;
  My heart with memory fills,
Of Nature in her loveliness,
  Amidst the granite hills.

THE TWO OFFERINGS.

The few sweet flowers I gave *last* May,
  Were bright and varied in their hue ;
The harbinger that summer's day
  And sunnier hours were coming too,
The fair face shone with sweet content,
  And lips and eyes were eloquent.

The few sweet flowers I give *this* May,
  Are pale and quiet in their hue ;
I drop them upon senseless clay,
  My last sad offering and — adieu.
The fair face lies in perfect rest,
The spirit with the truly blest.

But that was on the *first* of May,
  When living queens are crowned with
    flowers,
But now, poor May is nearly dead,
  With all its hoped for, sunny hours.

TO OUR SUMMER PARTY.

OUR pleasant group are scattering,
    That have passed the season here,
Like dried leaves that fall pattering,
    And are driven far and near.
In wantonness we 've dallied,
    Midst the sunshine and the showers,
With laughing voices rallied,
    Those who talked of fleeting hours.
But the summer days are going past,
    The autumn drawing near,
For the yellow leaves are showing fast
    The passing of the year.

We have climbed upon the mountains,
    And wandered through the vale,
And drank from Nature's fountains,
    While the wild bird trilled his tale,

To his mate in notes soft flowing,
  Of the places they would seek,
To sunnier climates going,
  When the days grew short and bleak.

We have watched the sun sink grandly
      down,
  Behind Chocorua's peak ;
The moon's first rays o'er Conway town,
  Rise tremblingly and weak ;
We have heard the loon's wild crying,
  As the stars began to shine,
And the balmy breeze came sighing,
  Down through the woods of pine.
But the summer days are going past,
  The autumn drawing near,
For the yellow leaves are showing fast,
  The passing of the year.

We have plucked the lilies from the lake,
  Clematis from the walls,
And followed where the clear streams take
  Their leaps o'er rocky falls.

The golden rod is bending,
  In the gentle August air,
The purple aster blending,
  With the green leaves everywhere.

Ah ! the summer is departing,
  With its wealth of sunny hours,
But the paths we tread at starting,
  Are still garlanded with flowers.
We will part with pleasant feeling,
  From these friends of summer days,
While regrets come o'er us stealing,
  As we wend our different ways,
While the summer days are going past,
  The autumn drawing near,
And the yellow leaves are showing fast,
  The passing of the year.

ISLIP.

Upon the waters of the lake,
  We sailed that sunny summer's day;
The light waves played on grassy banks,
  And sparkled with the emerald's ray.

The waters of the old South Bay,
  Lay in the distance clear and blue;
Fire Island's sands and towering light,
  And white sails gliding into view.

Gay parties walked upon the lawn,
  And laughing voices broke the air,
While Nature's raiment, washed by showers
  Shone in the sunlight fresh and fair.

We passed beneath the railroad span,
  And pushed up through the narrow
    stream,

While, startled from old mossy trunks,
 We broke the turtle's noon-day dream.

We picked the honeysuckle sweet,
 And bright wild roses from the stem;
But to the gentle maiden's eyes,
 White water-lilies formed the gem.

Out from the rippling waters deep,
 The speckled trout leaped up in play;
While down below like arrow shot,
 The pickerel on his rapid way.

The quail's shrill whistle clear we heard,
 The black crow flapped his lazy wing,
While from each waving bush or tree,
 The wild birds made their voices ring.

3

GIVE.

Of thy abundance give,
　　As thou hast store;
Help them who ask to live,
　　Only — no more.

Just as thou feelest right
　　Give to their need;
God of the widow's mite
　　Madest rich seed.

He alone knows the right;
　　We are but blind;
And in all powerful might,
　　Returns in kind.

AUTUMN.

THE luxury of autumn days is round us still :
    Upon the old rough bridge we idly sit,
On Nature at her rest we gaze at will,
    Drinking in memories we may not forget.

The aspen hardly flutters in the breeze,
    That scarce a ripple on the waters make ;
The bridge, rocks, mountains, all one sees,
    Reflected on the surface of the lake.

The hours, uncounted, slowly pass away,
    And minutes, hours, or ages, all to us are
      one,
And earth, itself, seemed dreaming as it lay,
    Bathed in the mellowness of that autumn
      sun.

All nature is inclined to indolence ;
    The slothful waters sleep upon the beach,

The very mountains shrink beneath the
    sense,
  Of added weight from fleecy clouds they
    reach.

The tinkling bells from far off, browsing
    kine,
  Comes softly stealing on the quiet ear;
The perfumed incense from the groves of
    pine,
  By noiseless footsteps rendered doubly
    dear.

In sleepy mood the purple daisies nod;
  Each bird has stolen to some quiet rest;
And, gorgeous in its dress, yon golden rod,
  Is leaning on that old rock's mossy breast.

We catch the slumberous spirit of the hour,
  And lay us down upon the piney sod,
And only dreamily we feel the power,
And wondrous beauties, of the Gracious
    God.

LITTLE ROUGH SHELLS.

LITTLE rough shells from the great salt sea,
Nothing of beauty to you may be,
Strung on a string by a lame old tar,
Gathered on shores near the Isle of Star.
Wonders they 've seen, child, that you or I,
Never can see with our human eye.
Lying still in the waters deep,
Or clinging to rocks, slimy and steep,
Way down deep midst a precious store,
Or flung on the beach with the tempest's
    roar ;
Beautiful minnows with filmy tail,
Have nibbled away at each lazy snail ;
Great green lobsters with pointed nose,
With crooked legs, and horny toes,
Have round them fought in savage wars,
With ponderous, curved, and snapping
    claws.

Above, the shark turned his opening maw,
To crunch his prey in his saw-set jaw,
The porpoise leaped from the waters high,
Till they thought *perhaps* he could touch
　　the sky;
Or the great whale floated his bulky length,
Or whipped the sea with his awful strength.
Wide-mouthed sculpins, in tawny dyes;
Moved around them with goggle eyes,
Wide-spread flounders, the slippery eel, —
A thousand wonders would around them
　　steal.
Or they slyly crept on the rocky ledge,
And reached the anemone's wondrous edge;
Hobnobbed with the oyster, raced with the
　　muscle,
While the crab and the sea-spider had a
　　tussle;
Oh! wonders they 've seen, child, that you
　　or I,
Never can see with our human eye.

O WONDROUS month, that watched the sum-
mer fight,
So valiantly against the chilly hosts of Fall,
Till, going to the garnered sunbeams of the
year,
Wild in its luxury it used them all.

The thousand mouths of glad old earth
drank in,
With copious draughts, the heated nectar
of the sun,
Till, reeling backward drunken with delight,
She dreamed that summer had but just
begun.

The perfect verdure of the full blown earth,
Each day was glorious in its green and
gold ;

The dazzling sun upon the Saco beamed,
  Till it in gilded ripples swiftly rolled.

The dome of Washington rose bright and
    clear,
  Or draperies transparent round it drew,
Changing its garments, without stint or fear,
  From sombre purple, to light gauzy blue.

Specked with brown acres, where the grain
    had grown,
  The lawn-like meadows still the elm trees
    shade,
Though buttercups and daisies all have
    flown,
  And madcap Bob-o-link to the south has
    strayed.

Flaunting his yellow crown with graceful
    air,
  And proudly bright, the golden rod stays
    still ;
And clustering round him modestly, yet fair,
  His sister asters bow before his will.

Then came October fighting for his own,
    Till weakly maples and the sumach bled
Ere Summer proudly placed him on his
       throne,
    Acknowledging to all that it was dead.

Deal kindly with thy victims, grim old Fall,
    For we have loved each leafy spray and
       spear;
Let them lie quiet till snow covers all,
    And winter turns to hail poor Nature's
       tear.

"NEVER TO BE FORGOTTEN."

Cords that are not easy broken,
  Frailest textures weave,
And words all too lightly spoken,
  Willing hearts believe.

Through long waiting days and years,
  Reaches that word "never,"
And in sorrow and in tears,
  Some hearts wait forever.

I might wish some planet bright,
  In the sky above me,
From its far-off realm of light,
  To come down and love me.

So, fair lady, in thy brightness
  If I seek a place,

Wilt thou treat the wish with lightness,
  Written in thy face?

If we do not meet for years,
  Wilt thou sweet thoughts treasure,
And of me, as I of thee,
  Always think with pleasure?

THE BAPTISM.

" I BAPTIZE thee " — and the water,
 Dropped upon the infant face,
And the baby look of wonder
 To a happy smile gave place.

Were there angel voices singing,
 Angel faces gathered near,
And the voices and the faces,
 It alone could see and hear?

" In the name of " — still the water,
 Trembled on the finger tips,
As the solemn words were uttered,
 Feelingly from hallowed lips.

" Father, Son, and Holy Ghost,"
 Softly on the air was spoken,

And the bright drops traced the cross,
Of Christ's followers the token.

Prayers invoked God's choicest blessings,
And the solemn rite closed when,
From the full hearts all responsive,
Came the meaning word, Amen.

THE COLLEGIATE CENTENNIAL REGATTA.

Saratoga Lake, July 19, 1876.

UNIVERSITY RACE.

THE sun shines hotly on the lake;
No grateful breeze the ripples make,
And in that heated summer air
Are crowds of men, and woman fair,
'Neath hanging flags, and colors bright,
Waiting impatiently the sight.
Three miles and more abreast " Snake Hill "
The rowers sit afloat but still,
Six boats by stalwart oarsmen manned,
By sun and weather brownly tanned,
With eager faces all aglow,
Wait anxiously the word to *Go.*
They 're off! and Cornell has the lead,
O'er waters smooth the light boats speed,

Pull, brothers of the shell and oar,
Pull as you never pulled before !
They who would pass that crew to-day
Must be no loiterers by the way,
For, coming upward on the lake,
You see their rapid lengthening wake,
Cornell still leading in the race,
And pulling for no second place.
Hark ! for a cry of " Harvard " grows,
Her crimson color faintly shows ;
Pull, Cambridge, for thy good old name,
Pull for thy half-forgotten fame,
Pull with the spirit brave and bold,
That won thee victories of old —
In vain ; with stroke they use so well,
Still in the front stays young Cornell.
A short time more, the work is done,
The white and red has victory won.
The crowd applaud with hearty cheers
The victors of the last two years.
Harvard comes in for second place ;
Columbia's sons three in the race ;
Then Union, Princeton, Wesleyans make,
The finish at the judge's stake.

Strong-handed and brave-hearted crews,
Who on their merits win or lose.
Oh, manlier far to strive and fail,
Than shun the venture as did Yale.
No victors' crowns would rust with you,
Won when competitors were few;
In this our great Centennial year,
You showed no craven face of fear.
So let the race of life be run,
And victory crown work nobly done.

SINGLE SCULL RACE.

Again the cannon down the lake,
The single sculls their places take;
And now they also forward dart,
Cornell again leads at the start,
And as before it wins the race,
With Harvard in its second place.

Lastly, the freshman crews compete,
To make the college day complete;
Again Cornell, midst thundering cheers,
The winner of this race appears,
And, leading from the judges' boat,
They, crowned with laurels, gayly float.

Glory enough; the winners they,
Of all the honors of the day;
Let Ithaca resound with noise,
Over her sun-burnt hardy boys,
And old Cayuga proudly bear,
The colors that her navies wear.

4

ON THE WHITE MOUNTAIN DAISY.

Sweet little flower, whose dress of modest
    white,
The eyes of tired mountaineers delight,
Seeking to find the warmth of summer
    skies,
When chilly winter's snow in summer lies,
We take thee with us, in a tender hope,
That some new buds may in our summer
    ope.

You may be dazzled by the brighter blaze,
That in our lowlands warmer sunlight plays,
And in its very warmth of luxury die,
While we look down on thee with pitying
    eye.
Forgive the hand that loving dared to seek,
To win thee to us from the mountain peak.

And even then you may not die in vain ;
Some straying seed may rise above the
    plain,
And toiling up thy native mountain slow,
May reach its comrades in the falling
    snow,
And tell some storm-toss'd, doubtful, shiver-
    ing mate
That theirs is not a really dismal fate,

Who on a toil-worn passing traveler's face,
Calls forth a smile amidst the dreariest
    place,
Who in their humble life do but their
    duty,
May to some others be a thing of beauty ;
Who raise a truthful face to look above,
May turn the bitterest heart to thoughts of
    love.

Then live thy life amongst the lofty rocks,
That grimly bear the fiercest winter shocks,

And patient wait, to please some wanderer's
    eye,
Whose weary feet have crossed the mount-
    ains high.
Thy gentle face raise to the changing sun,
O pretty daisy of Mount Washington.

OUR SHIP IS IN.

OUR ship is in! our ship is in!
   From off the wintry seas;
The pennons from her towering masts
   Wave gayly in the breeze.

We've bravely hoped through stormy years,
   And watched the coming sails,
And mournful gazed, while other hopes,
   Were foundered in the gales.

And now with quiet folded arms,
   We sit upon her decks,
And, wondering, think upon the fate,
   That kept her from the wrecks.

Now, almost driven on the rocks,
   That thrust their threatening heads,
As if they sought to lay her ribs,
   Among their stony beds.

How hard to keep the way through storms,
  How sharp the lightnings flashed,
As answering to the wind's fierce roar,
  The awful thunders crashed.

How pleasant sailed we summer days,
  How near the harbor seemed,
How softly blew the gentle wind,
  How bright the waters gleamed.

But chilling mists would round us fall,
  The winds would backward blow,
And toilsome was the way to port,
  And time was all too slow.

But we have conquered storms and waves,
  Look back without a sigh,
And joyfully upon the air,
  We fling our banners high.

THE BIRTHDAY.

LITTLE Julia's birthday 's here ;
Our best wishes to the dear,
Little, merry, dancing sprite,
Household's pleasure and delight.
 Full of frolic and of play,
 She 's just four years old to-day.

Bright black eyes with mischief teeming,
Face like those of artist's dreaming,
Winning easily our hearts,
By her little childish arts.
 Full of frolic and of play,
 And she 's four years old to-day.

Blessings on thy darling head ;
Pleasant be the paths you tread ;
May you have " a ittle tiss "
Always, when you need the bliss.
 May thy heart in future stay,
 Free from trouble as to-day.

TO MISS B——, ON HER FAN.

COME, kindliest spirits of the air,
    And make of this your choicest resting-
       place;
In all your realms you'll press no form
       more fair,
    And call the roses to no sweeter face.

I'll envy you each gentle touch you steal
    Among the tresses of her soft brown hair,
And on her lips and brow you can but feel
    The mortal sweetness ever lingering there.

I'll chide you not, if mortal-like you'd stay,
    And linger ever 'mongst the charms I see,
If, in her softest moods, you sometimes may,
    With gentlest breezes, bring sweet
       thoughts of me.

TO MISS ——.

Oh, that maiden of sixteen,
Fairest of the fair I ween!
I am in a dangerous way,
Though my hairs *are* getting gray,
Though I'm bound by other ties,
And it should be otherwise.

They have put me very near,
This enchanting little dear;
Morning, noon, and eventide,
I am seated by her side,
And those eyes of purest blue,
Have the power to pierce one through.

And the oval face so fair,
And her waving light brown hair, —
How can I escape from harm,
Placed each day beside the charm?

How can I escape the while,
From the sweetness of her smile?

Spare me, gentle maid, I pray,
While I serve thee every day;
Let those blue ensnaring eyes,
Seize upon some other prize;
  will grateful homage give,
To the latest day I live.

TO MISS McQ——.

FAIR lady in this quiet town,
　　Who strangely moves these *hearts* of
　　　　ours,
Would I could weave some fitting crown,
　　To note the magic of thy powers.

They go with you where'er you will,
　　They have no power, they know no choice,
They bow in woe, with joy they thrill,
　　All at the summons of thy voice.

Sing of the past, and memory treads,
　　With silent feet its backward ways,
And ties again the broken threads,
　　That lead us to those by-gone days.

Sing of the future, with its hopes,
　　Its bows of promise, bright and fair,
And lo! the golden gateway opes,
　　To gilded castles in the air;

Of love, and manly hearts beat high,
  In chords responsive to thine own;
Of sorrow, and the smothered sigh,
  Tells of some grief we all have known.

Farewell!   May friends throughout thy life,
  Like thy sweet notes, prove ever true;
Whate'er may come of joy, or strife,
  Undimmed by tears those eyes of blue.

TO MISS M——.

THE sun is setting, and its rays forgetting
   All but the brightest of the objects here;
On one it hovers as they were lovers,
   Among the many that are gathered near.

We do not wonder that the sun should lin-
      ger,
   Among the mazes of thy beauteous hair,
And only that the *world itself* turned over,
   Could it be kept from ever resting there.

TO A YOUNG GIRL.

THY birthday must not pass unnoticed by
    Among the mountains,
Where we are seeking rest, or drinking
    health,
    From purest fountains.
We all admire thy graceful ways, sweet
    child,
And see another joy, amidst nature wild.

A young, fair face ; a true, pure girlish heart
    Full of affection,
That will bring ever loving thoughts of thee
    To recollection.
Bright promise of a tender woman's life,
Quick to enjoy, strong if it must meet strife.

We would not have thee miss one drop of
    bliss,
    Or earthly pleasure,

Or have thee lose one real ringing coin,
    From out thy treasure.
Taste to the utmost all thou canst of joy,
Let all but be *unmixed* with base alloy.

But as thine eyes at sunset on the peaks,
    See still a glory,
That of unending day beyond your sight,
    Tells you the story,
And makes thee wish that you could reach
    the height,
And look beyond the darkness into light,

So may thy heart be ever looking up,
    Beyond this living ;
While still enjoying all of life it may,
    Be ever giving,
Itself to one who, when the end is near,
Will place thee, crowned, 'midst glories ever
    clear.

TO THE MISSES S——.

Farewell ! no more the painted boat,
With fair-haired girls will gently float,
    Moved by their wayward oar ;
Their hands with loving clasp will take,
No lilies from Pequauket Lake,
    This summer season more.

No more their longing eyes will seek,
The summit of the mountain's peak,
    While toiling upward slow.
The mosses of the rocks will greet,
No more this year their roving feet,
    As pleasuring they go.

Farewell ! we wish thy paths may be,
Through life as smooth as here we see,
    The waters of the lake ;
Thy onward steps may reach the height,
Where all is peace, and love, and light,
    The rest we all would take.

TO M——.

Maiden, fair as flowers in May,
Like the sunshine of this day,
Like the brightness round us beaming,
Like these flowers with sweetness teeming,
Deign to let some truant ray,
From thy presence round me stray,
Even though I felt its power,
To my very latest hour.

5

FOR FANNIE D——'s ALBUM.

I DEDICATE this book to thee ;
   Each opening page will bear,
A token that some loving friend,
   Has left with pleasure there.

A trembling line, a hurried word,
   Affection bade them write,
To bid thee to remember them,
   As oft they catch thy sight.

In after years full many a tear,
   Methinks, may dim thine eye,
As on that leaf some friend has traced
   To thee, their last good-by.

Or as some well-remembered verse,
   Calls up to memory's view,
The last sad earthly parting 'twixt,
   That loving friend and you.

And thou wilt prize it, Fannie dear,
    As a most precious gem,
The last, the dear connecting link,
    That's left 'tween thee and them.

Or thou wilt smile as thou dost turn,
    Its different pages o'er,
And recollection brings to mind
    Some merry day of yore.

Or now, with half-averted eye,
    Thou 'lt read some tender line,
From one who tells thee he adores,
    Each word, thought, look of thine.

Brother and sister, lover, friend,
    Playmates of youthful days,
As slowly o'er and o'er thou turnest,
    Will meet thine earnest gaze.

And, Fannie, like this little book,
    As page by page 't is turned,
Shows forth on each some cherished friend,
    Towards whom your bosom burned,

So may thy life, as day by day,
    Time gently turns a leaf,
And warns while yet he bids rejoice,
    Though sweet, it yet is brief,

Add for each one a new found friend,
    Some warm and kindly heart,
That time or absence will not chill,
    And but with life depart.

And may that life be all of joy,
    All beautifully bright,
And heaven be near thee as this earth,
    Fades gently from thy sight.

TO FLORENCE ON HER BIRTHDAY.

DEAR child, we greet thee ;
Kind friends here meet thee ;
With wishes we strew thy way.
   Nature is beaming,
   Sunlight is streaming,
All round thy footsteps to-day.

Come forth, Florence bright !
Cried the morning light,
They say you are eleven.
   An answering sound,
   Came from all around,
Under the bright, blue heaven.

Eleven 's the youth,
Speaks out upright truth,

As she sits majestic, fair,
  And her clear, cold cry,
  Rose up far and high,
Away into upper air.

And the leaves all green,
And bright flowers I ween,
Dressed out in their summer hue,
  With their lisping tongue,
  Cried, "So fair and young,
Why, Florence, it must be you!"

"Eleven, now mind,"
Says the rushing wind,
And his voice sounds loud and bold,
  And roused by the shock,
  From his cave of rock,
Comes tremblingly Echo old.

"Eleven's Florence,"
Babbled the torrents,

As they go surging and wild,
  But sweet spirits near,
  Ask " Eleven ? Come here,
And sit on these mosses, child.

" We will bathe thy brow,
  If it 's heated now,
With nectar will moisten thy lip,
  Till all spirits long,
  In their secret song,
A taste of its sweets to sip."

So with spirits rare,
With all bright and fair,
We fain would weave thee a spell
  That would reach from here,
  To that brighter sphere,
And thy soul said, " All is well."

TO MRS. ——.

AND thou would'st deign to ask a line from
    me?
  And, as I look, there comes that soft sweet
    smile,
That ever on thy face I long to see,
  That make me wish that I could change
    the while,
    With that fair boy,
Who clinging round thee, turns his eyes
    above,
And meets thy looks of love,
    With one of joy.

No! ask it not, for better men than *I*,
  Are neither cold as stone nor hard as steel,
Might dare to love an *angel*, were one nigh,
  And tempted, tell that angel what they feel,
    And risk the scorn,

That meant to tear such feelings from their
　　　place,
Would only make them wish that angel
　　　face,
　　More human born.

TO MRS. E——.

Dear woman from the far-off West,
One can but feel that he is blest,
When that which is a pleasant task,
You as a favor deign to ask.

In after years, I fain would still,
Some pleasant place in memory fill,
When in thy mind remembered plays,
The happy hours of vanished days.

Large-hearted, formed in generous mold,
Thy metal has the ring of gold;
Thy happy laugh and cheerful ways
Have been the gilding of these days.

We look into thy pleasant face,
And naught unworthy finds a place;
No envy, hate, or malice lies,
Within those clear blue honest eyes.

You need no praise from lips of mine,
When daily round thy footsteps shine,
The noblest words to crown a life,
Of faithful daughter, mother, wife.

OUR NATIONAL CENTENNIAL JUBILEE,

JULY 4, 1876.

ALL hail, our great centennial day !
 Let forty million souls
Join in the hallelujah,
 That o'er the nation rolls.

Let every heart be filled with joy,
 And every tongue give praise,
And with a nation's gratitude,
 A nation's anthem raise,

To thank the power that saved us,
 In our struggling feeble years,
The patriot band, that fought the fight,
 And laughed at coward fears.

God bless the glorious stars and stripes
 That proudly waves in air ;

God bless the patriotic hearts,
  That kept it flying there.

We are welcoming all nations,
  From the farthest ends of earth,
To join in the rejoicings,
  Of our first centennial birth.

From Asia and from China,
  From Turkey and Japan,
From the frozen zones that whiten
  To the burning suns that tan;

From Austria and from Spain's fair land,
  Of the olive and the dance;
From Russia and from Germany,
  From laughing " La belle France; "

And brave old Mother England's sons,
  Of science and of toil,
Have come to view the wonders,
  That spring from Yankee soil.

How show to them our country,
   Its progress and its strength,
The changes that one hundred years,
   Have made throughout its length.

From where Auroras gayly dye,
   The frosted air of Arctic sky,
To southern sun, whose torrid beams,
   On gulf and mainland fiercely gleams.

East where Atlantic's tempests roar,
   West to Pacific's golden shore, —
A land a nation well may love,
   With Freedom's banner streaming o'er.

No slave within our borders,
   No tyrant in the land,
And man is noble only,
   As his nature makes him grand.

Our railroads span the continent,
   North, south, from east to west,
O'er mountain pass and prairie wide,
   The rapid engine knows no rest.

Born of a native's fertile brain,
　　Far stretch the telegraphic wires;
With magic voice its tips are touched,
　　Fed by the swift electric fires.

The throbbing of the paddles,
　　Sound on rivers, and on lakes;
Unnumbered workshops ringing,
　　With the music labor makes.

Free to all youth, the rich, the poor,
　　Our schools dot hill and dell;
The freedom of religious thought,
　　The thousand church-spires tell.

Land of the cotton, and the corn,
　　Of orange groves and northern pines,
Of prairies rich to feed the world,
　　Of coal, and precious mines!

Oh, will another hundred years
　　Thy further progress show,
To set, as now, all patriot hearts
　　With native pride aglow?

Upward, and onward, be thy course;
Work, brave hearts, as you must;
With brighter glow the motto shine,
The words "In God we trust."

OUR FLAG CENTENNIAL.

JUNE, 1877.

THROW out thy graceful folds, O flag,
  Upon the bright June air!
As when a century ago, :
  A nation placed thee there.
'T was done 'midst benisons and tears ;
      No coward fears,
The emblem of a land to be,
      Forever free.

Throw out thy graceful folds, O flag!
  Faint shone thy stars, I ween,
When first upon thy azure field,
  Were wrought the old thirteen.
Few were thy bannered armies then,
      But they were — men,
And bravely, 'neath their country's pride,
      Fought side by side.

6

Throw out thy graceful folds, O flag,
  Thy stars have multiplied!
And Freedom's rays shine brightly forth,
  O'er land and ocean wide.
But once, thy armies fought with pain,
      Yet not in vain,
Though through our country's blood-soaked
    sod,
      Thou 'rt saved, thank God.

Throw out thy graceful folds, O flag,
  From mountain peaks and dells!
Shout forth huzzahs o'er all the land,
  Ring out with joy, ye bells ;
Our flag has waved through hopes and fears,
      One hundred years.
Oh ! may it float upon the breeze,
      For centuries !

Throw out thy graceful folds, O flag,
  High in the bright June air!
And let a mighty nation bow,
  Below in grateful prayer.

God keep beneath red, white, and blue,
    A nation true;
Upholding with its powerful might,
    Only the right.

THE NORTH TO THE SOUTH, 1866.

THE war is past, and now no more,
We hear the cruel cannon's roar;
No more we listen to the crash,
Of bayonet, or sabre's clash,
The Angel Peace, with tear-stained eyes,
Looks o'er the land in glad surprise.

The olden sun in glory shines,
On northern rocks, and southern vines;
The self-same clouds drop silent tears,
On northern graves and southern biers;
One hallowed flag waves over all
That sprang at north, or southern's call;
And one just God, with pitying eye,
Sees where our buried passions lie.

We ask not if your hands are red,
With blood of northern honored dead;

We mourn with you when tears you shed,
O'er southern hearts that freely bled ;
We stretch an honest hand to you ;
Oh take it, with a grasp as true.

THE NATION'S PRAYER.

MARCH 4, 1877.

O Thou, who rul'st in majesty above,
Look down, we beg, in mercy, and with
love
On him who reverently, with bended knee,
Asks us to join in humble prayer to Thee.

O Thou, who only hast the power to
guide,
Let him in Thee with perfect trust abide;
Be Thou his counselor, be Thou his friend,
And let Thy blessing upon him descend.

And as he takes his solemn oath this day,
And lifts the burden for the weary way,
May he find favor in the nation's sight,
And may that nation, make his burden
light.

Be strife and discord banished from our soil,
Our laurels gathered those of friendly toil ;
And peace and plenty smile o'er all our
 land,
And all the people own Thy fostering hand.